PICKLE THINGS
To librarians, parents, and teachers:

Pickle Things is a Parents Magazine READ ALOUD
Original — one title in a series of colorfully illustrated
and fun-to-read stories that young readers will be
sure to come back to time and time again.

Now, in this special school and library edition of
Pickle Things, adults have an even greater
opportunity to increase children's responsiveness to
reading and learning — and to have fun every step of
the way.

When you finish this story, check the special section
at the back of the book. There you will find games,
projects, things to talk about, and other educational
activities designed to make reading enjoyable by
giving children and adults a chance to play together,
work together, and talk over the story they have
just read.

Parents Magazine READ ALOUD Originals:

Golly Gump Swallowed a Fly	Henry's Important Date
The Housekeeper's Dog	Elephant Goes to School
Who Put the Pepper in the Pot?	Rabbit's New Rug
Those Terrible Toy-Breakers	Sand Cake
The Ghost in Dobbs Diner	Socks for Supper
The Biggest Shadow in the Zoo	The Clown-Arounds Go on Vacation
The Old Man and the Afternoon Cat	The Little Witch Sisters
Septimus Bean and His Amazing Machine	The Very Bumpy Bus Ride
Sherlock Chick's First Case	Henry Babysits
A Garden for Miss Mouse	There's No Place Like Home
Witches Four	Up Goes Mr. Downs
Bread and Honey	Bicycle Bear
Pigs in the House	Sweet Dreams, Clown-Arounds!
Milk and Cookies	The Man Who Cooked for Himself
But No Elephants	Where's Rufus?
No Carrots for Harry!	The Giggle Book
Snow Lion	Pickle Things
Henry's Awful Mistake	Oh, So Silly!
The Fox with Cold Feet	The Peace-and-Quiet Diner
Get Well, Clown-Arounds!	Ten Furry Monsters
Pets I Wouldn't Pick	One Little Monkey
Sherlock Chick and the Giant	The Silly Tail Book
Egg Mystery	Aren't You Forgetting Something, Fiona?
Cats! Cats! Cats!	

Library of Congress Cataloging-in-Publication Data

Brown, Marc Tolon.
    Pickle things / by Marc Brown.
       p. cm. -- (Parents magazine read aloud original)
    "North American library edition"--T.p. verso.
    Summary: Describes, in rhymed text and illustrations, all the many things that a pickle isn't.
    ISBN 0-8368-0985-8
    [1. Pickles--Fiction. 2. Stories in rhyme.] I. Title. II. Series.
    PZ8.3.B8147Pi 1994
    [E]--dc20   93-36125

This North American library edition published in 1994 by Gareth Stevens Publishing, 1555 North RiverCenter Drive, Suite 201, Milwaukee, Wisconsin 53212, USA, under an arrangement with Parents Magazine Press, New York.

Text and illustrations © 1980 by Marc Brown. Portions of end matter adapted from material first published in the newsletter *From Parents to Parents* by the Parents Magazine Read Aloud Book Club, © 1990 by Gruner + Jahr, USA, Publishing; other portions © 1994 by Gareth Stevens, Inc.

Printed in the United States of America

1 2 3 4 5 6 7 8 9 99 98 97 96 95 94

by Marc Brown

Gareth Stevens Publishing
Milwaukee

Parents Magazine Press
New York

FOR:
TOLON AND TUCKER
TWO SWEET PICKLES

Pickle things you never see . . .
Like pickles on a Christmas tree.

A pickle ear,

a pickle nose,

pickle hair,

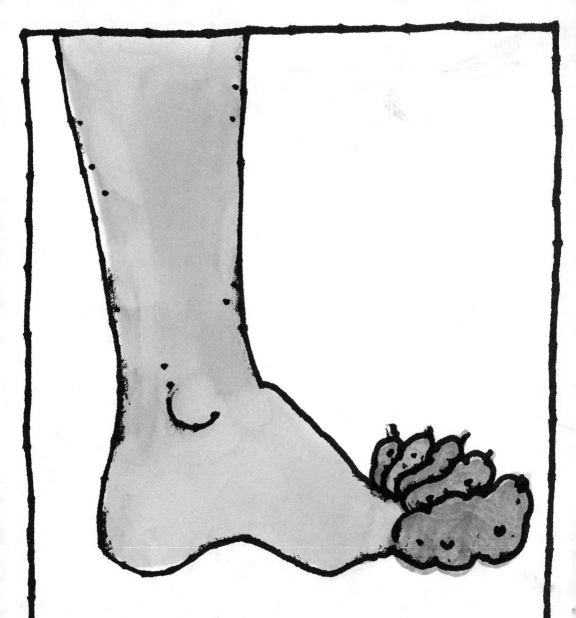

and pickle toes.

Pickle up,
pickle down,
juggled by a pickle clown.

Pickle in,

pickle out,

pickles from the waterspout.

Pickle
things
you
never
make . . .

Like pickle pie

and pickle cake.

Pickle donuts,

pickle flakes,

pickle candies,

pickle shakes.

Pickle things you never buy...

Like pickle kites
that fly sky high.

A pickle ball,
a pickle bat,

a pickle train,
a pickle hat.

You never hear a pickle talk.

You never see a pickle walk.

You never hear a pickle sing.

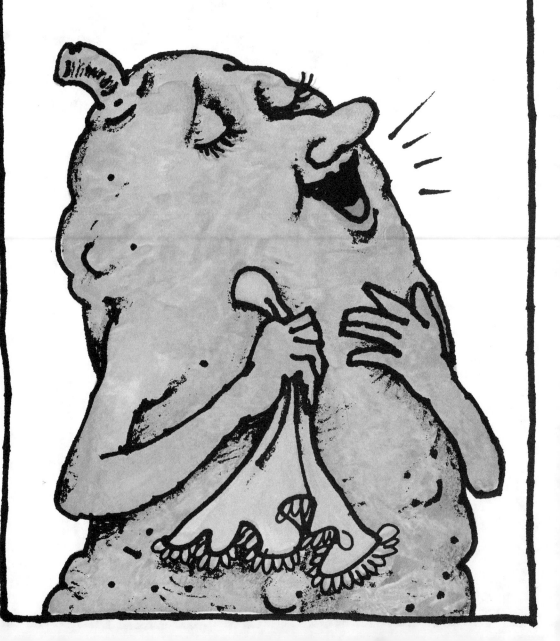

Or see a pickle leave a ring.

Can you ride a pickle boat around a pickle-castle moat?

Or ever steer a pickle bike
down pickle street and pickle pike?

Or ever fly a pickle plane
through pickle snow
and pickle rain?

Or ski a pickle down a slope?

Or
climb
a pickle
with a
rope?

One thing for sure you never do
is wear a pickle for a shoe.
Never pickles on your feet...

Of course not, silly,
THEY'RE TO EAT!

Notes to Grown-ups

Major Themes

Here is a quick guide to the significant themes and concepts at work in *Pickle Things:*

- Imagination: taking a common, everyday object and seeing many different (and silly!) things in it.
- Rhyming fun: the author's simple, delightful rhymes are ideal tools for beginning readers.

Step-by-step Ideas for Reading and Talking

Here are some ideas for further give-and-take between grown-ups and children. The following topics encourage creative discussion of *Pickle Things* and invite the kind of open-ended response that is consistent with many contemporary approaches to reading, including Whole Language:

- Rhymes are perfect for reading aloud. A beginning reader can hear and see how rhyming words differ from, or are similar to, each other, and the components — syllables — that make them so.
- There's a surprising variety of silly things in *Pickle Things*, and they all involve pickles. Can your child think of anything more? Try a different object: soap (for soapy things), water (for soggy things), etc.
- While it's always important to keep in mind the needs of a beginning reader, it's sometimes just as important to sit back with your child, put thoughts about reading readiness aside, and just enjoy a good book together. But don't worry: your "time off" will still be productive for your youngster, who will see a book used in a relaxing, enjoyable setting. And that can be the best reading lesson of all.

Games for Learning

Games and activities can stimulate young readers and listeners alike to find out more about words, numbers, and ideas. Here are more ideas for turning learning into fun:

Picklesicles

Pickles are definitely to be eaten, and on a hot day, a nice, cool pickle can really hit the spot. But how about a *really* hot day? That's when you need a cooler than cold, delicious and bold pickle. In fact, you need a picklesicle!

Picklesicle recipe:

You will need:

- as many Popsicle sticks as you want picklesicles (5 or 10 will be plenty).
- as many pickles as you have sticks (sweet gherkins and kosher dills are recommended, but if you have a different favorite, that will do nicely).
- a plastic container large enough to lay your picklesicles in, side by side.
- room in your freezer for the plastic container.

To assemble: Help your child stick the end of a Popsicle stick into one end of each pickle. If they are very firm pickles, you may want to use a small knife to get the hole started for your child's stick. Set the picklesicles in the plastic container. Set the box in the freezer and wait two hours or until a really hot day. Then slurp and chomp the tangy picklesicles.

About the Author/Artist

MARC BROWN tries out many of his books on the children he visits in schools across the country — as well as on his own two sons. He is always eager to share their enthusiasm and listen carefully to their suggestions, which he feels has helped his growth as a writer and illustrator.

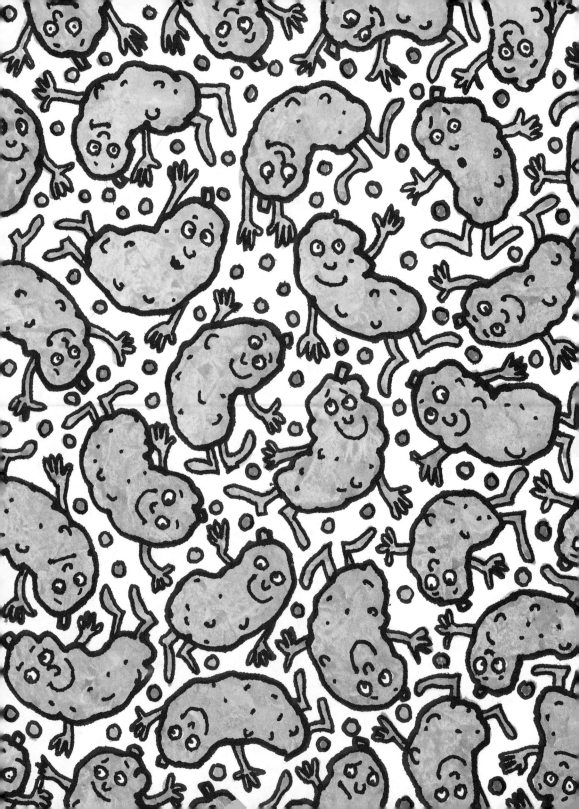